Here's a list of all the
Redfeather Books from Henry Holt

The Fourth-Grade Four
by Marilyn Levinson

Monstra Vs. Irving
by Stephen Manes

Something Special
by Emily Rodda

Weird Wolf
by Margery Cuyler

MONSTRA *vs.* IRVING

Stephen Manes

MONSTRA

vs.

IRVING

Illustrated by Michael Sours

A REDFEATHER BOOK

Henry Holt and Company • New York

Published by Henry Holt and Company, Inc.,
115 West 18th Street, New York, New York 10011.
Published in Canada by Fitzhenry & Whiteside Limited,
195 Allstate Parkway, Markham, Ontario L3R 4T8.

Library of Congress Cataloging-in-Publication Data
Manes, Stephen.
    Monstra vs. Irving / Stephen Manes : illustrated by Michael Sours.
        (Redfeather books)
    Summary: Irving's plans to scare his bratty little sister Claire
backfire when she drinks his mail-order magic potion and is
transformed into a monster.
    ISBN 0-8050-0836-5
    [1. Monsters—Fiction. 2. Magic—Fiction. 3. Brothers and
sisters—Fiction.] I. Sours, Michael, ill. II. Title.
III. Title: Monstra versus Irving. IV. Series.
PZ7.M31264Mo   1989
[E]—dc20   89-33423

Henry Holt books are available at special discounts
for bulk purchases for sales promotions, premiums,
fund-raising, or educational use. Special editions
or book excerpts can also be created to specification.

    For details contact:

    Special Sales Director
    Henry Holt and Company, Inc.
    115 West 18th Street
    New York, New York 10011

First Edition
Designed by Maryann Leffingwell
Printed in the United States of America
10 9 8 7 6 5 4 3 2 1

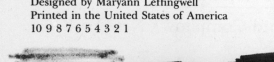

MONSTRA *vs.* IRVING

1

Everybody thought Claire Shapiro was cute — everybody but Claire's brother Irving.

Irving didn't think she was cute at all. Irving thought she was a monster.

Claire was always doing something horrible—and giggling about it. It drove Irving crazy.

Claire stole his very best pen. And giggled.

Claire jumped up and down on his bed and messed it up. And giggled.

Claire swiped the very last piece of cake and stuffed it in her pocket. And giggled.

Claire scribbled a picture all over the back of Irving's spelling homework. And giggled.

Claire broke the wing off Irving's model jumbo jet. And giggled.

But Irving could never seem to get even. He couldn't yell at Claire, because then his parents would yell at *him* for yelling at his little sister. He couldn't beat her up, because then he'd get into big trouble. And he didn't really want to beat her up anyway. All he wanted to do was make her quit bothering him.

Everything he tried just backfired. When he jumped up and down on *her* bed, Claire hollered so loud he had to hold his hands over his ears. When he stole *her* pen, she shrieked so loud it hurt his teeth. And both times his parents scolded him for upsetting his little sister.

"It's not fair," Irving told his parents. "When I do something wrong, I get in trouble. When the little monster does something wrong, you just think it's cute."

Claire giggled. She *was* cute—when she wasn't being a monster.

Mrs. Shapiro sighed. "Just try to get along with your little sister, okay?"

"Please?" Mr. Shapiro said.

"Okay," said Irving. "But from now on I'm calling her Monstra."

"Don't," said Mrs. Shapiro.

Claire just giggled.

2

"Look what my brother gave me!" said Irving's friend Pete the next day. It was the very first issue of *Monsters Illustrated* magazine. Pete set it down carefully on Irving's bed.

"Neat!" Irving said. Pete's older brother gave Pete lots of great stuff. The only thing Claire had ever given Irving was chicken pox.

Pete pointed to the cover. " 'Thorblog the Swamp Mutant,' " he read. " 'Only an atomic bomb can stop him!' "

"Sounds just like my little sister," Irving joked.

Pete handed him the magazine. "Be careful. This may be valuable someday."

Irving flipped through the pages. "Here's a monster that even looks like my sister," Irving said. "Only not as cute."

Suddenly there was a loud noise out in the hallway.

"What was that?" Pete asked.

"Probably my sister. Monstra herself," Irving said. "Don't pay her any attention. Hey, look at this ad!"

Pete and Irving read it together. On the left there was a picture of a normal-looking kid and the word BEFORE. On the right was a picture of a really scary monster and the word AFTER. Pete and Irving read the headline out loud: " 'Monster-Ade makes *you* a real monster!' "

There was an even louder noise out in the hall. "Aren't you going to see what's going on?" Pete asked.

"No," said Irving. "It'll just get me in trouble."

Pete poked his head out the door. "Hey, Irving, are there supposed to be little plastic peanuts all over the hall?"

Irving rushed over. It was true, all right. Claire was rolling around in a sea of plastic packing peanuts—the ones he'd been saving in a garbage bag in the garage for a science project. They were all over the hall. They were a mess. And Irving knew he'd be the one who'd have to clean them up.

"Go into your room! Now!" he growled at Claire. Claire just giggled.

Irving shook his fist at her. Claire giggled some more.

Irving tried to chase her, but he slipped on the pellets. Claire ran into her room and slammed the door.

Pete looked at the mess and shook his head.

"That sister of yours really is a monster."

Irving just sighed and went back into his bedroom. He picked up Pete's magazine and pointed to the advertisement.

"You know who needs this Monster-Ade stuff?" he said. "Me!"

3

"Think about it," Irving said. "Wouldn't it be great? If I were really a monster, I could chase Claire around. She'd *have* to listen to me. She couldn't get away with *anything*."

Pete smiled. "I'll say! It'd be perfect, that's all!"

Irving and Pete read the advertisement:

> DON'T JUST READ ABOUT MONSTERS!
> **Be** one! Just one taste of Monster-Ade, and you **will** be—in seconds!
>
> **Monster-Ade** begins with a special blend of expensive ingredients and adds the latest in modern potion technology. It's the **state of the art** in **TRANSMOGRIFICATION!**

"What does 'transmogrification' mean?" Irving asked Pete.

"Changing from one thing to another."

"Where'd you learn that?" Irving asked.

"When it comes to monsters, I know everything," Pete replied.

"Well, I have got to get some of this stuff," Irving said. He read on:

> Best of all, **Monster-Ade** lets YOU decide how monstrous to become! Take one sip, and you'll discover how delicious being a monster can be. Drink a whole glass, and you'll be a monster for days!

"I don't need just a glassful," said Irving. "I need a whole bottle. A quart. A gallon."

"Not at these prices!" Pete stuck his finger on the coupon at the bottom of the ad:

> **ORDER NOW!** Comes complete with enough powder for one big glass, plus antidote! **Just $8.99,** plus $1.01 postage and handling. Send to: **Monster-Ade Technology**, Box 106, Transylvania, KY 40044.
>
> Allow two to four weeks for delivery.

"Ten dollars!" Irving exclaimed. "For one glass!"

"You also get the antidote," Pete remarked. "That's what turns you back into a human again."

"It's an awful lot of money," Irving said thoughtfully.

Pete was sure Irving would say "Forget it!" He was positive Irving would say "What a gyp!"

But Irving didn't. He just shrugged and said, "I'm going to order some anyway."

Irving went over to his desk and picked up his robotic-arm bank. When you put a coin in the robotic hand, the robotic arm dropped the money in a little slot.

But Irving wasn't going to put money in. He was going to take money out. He opened the bank with a key. He stuck his fingers in. He rooted around inside the bank. Finally he took out a ten-dollar bill.

"Come on," Pete said. "You're crazy if you spend it on this. I bet it's all a gyp. A swindle. They'll send you some plain old regular soft drink. And it'll say if you want to be a monster, run around growling. Or something."

But Irving had made up his mind. "Let me clip out that coupon."

"Are you kidding? This issue may be a collector's item someday. I'm not going to let you cut holes in it."

"Then keep the dumb old coupon. I'll just write to them without it."

"What if it really is a swindle? What if they take your money and don't send you anything? What if the stuff doesn't work?"

"I'll take my chances," Irving replied.

Pete handed Irving the magazine. He opened it up and stared at the "after" part of the ad again. He loved the idea of being able to boss little Monstra around. It really would be the perfect revenge.

"I'm telling you, you'll be sorry," Pete said. "It's never going to work."

Irving took an envelope out of his desk and wrote the company's name and address on it. Then he took out a sheet of notebook paper. "Please send me some Monster-Ade," he wrote. "Fast!" Below that he wrote his name and address.

Irving put the paper in the envelope. He put a stamp on the envelope. He took one last look at his ten-dollar bill.

"That's a lot of money," Pete said. "You said so yourself. You sure you really want to do this?"

Irving sighed. He put the bill in the envelope and sealed it shut. Then he went up the street and dropped it in the mailbox before Pete could make him change his mind.

4

Claire did a lot of monstrous things and a lot of giggling that week and the next. But Irving didn't so much as holler at her. Even his parents noticed. "You've been very good with Claire lately," his mother said one night at dinner. "We're proud of you."

Claire giggled. And when Irving thought of what was in store for her, he couldn't help giggling a little himself.

Every day when he came home from school, Irving rushed to the mailbox to see what was inside. But after two weeks had gone by, there was still no package from Transylvania, Kentucky.

Irving began to worry. Pete was probably right. He was never going to get any Monster-Ade at all. The Monster-Ade company was just going to steal his money. He might as well forget about it.

But he couldn't forget about it. He was thinking about it one afternoon when his sister sneaked into his room. She grabbed his baseball glove—the one personally autographed by Willie Flashner—and ran away.

Irving chased her into her bedroom. He could overlook a lot of things, but messing with his personally autographed baseball glove wasn't one of them.

Claire threw the glove into the corner behind her bed.

"You just wait," Irving told her as he picked it up. "You'll see what happens to monsters like you."

Claire just stuck her tongue out and giggled. But as Irving picked up his glove, he noticed something underneath it. It was a little box wrapped in plain brown paper. It was addressed to him. It was from Transylvania, Kentucky.

Irving exploded. "Where did you get this?"

Claire just giggled.

"How long have you had it?"

Claire just giggled.

Irving shook his finger at her. "Monstra, if you—" Then he stopped short. Why bother? In a few minutes he'd be a real monster. In a few minutes she'd be so scared, she'd never bother him again.

Irving giggled and walked out the door.

5

Irving took the box into his room. He opened it carefully. Monster-Ade was too expensive to waste a drop.

Inside the box were two clear cellophane packets. One packet was marked ANTIDOTE. It had red crystals inside. The other packet had green crystals. It was marked *Monster-Ade!* WARNING! DO NOT USE UNTIL YOU READ IN-STRUCTIONS.

The instructions said:

Thank you for purchasing **Monster-Ade**, the world's leading transmogrification potion. Please take a moment to read these simple instructions:

1. Mix each packet well with one cup (eight ounces) of water.

2. A little **Monster-Ade** goes a long way! Try a small amount at a time. Stop when you reach the level of monstrousness you desire.

3. To stop being a monster, drink the antidote. Be sure to drink at least as much as you drank of **Monster-Ade**. In seconds you should return to normal.

REMEMBER: Green means Go *(Monster-Ade)*.
Red means Stop (antidote).

Always make sure the antidote is nearby when you
drink *Monster-Ade*. **Never** drink *Monster-Ade* un-
less you have the antidote ready. *Monster-Ade* Tech-
nology **will not be responsible** for any accidents that
happen if you fail to follow this simple rule!

Irving grinned. Would Pete be surprised! Not
to mention Claire! This was going to be great!

Irving took the Monster-Ade package to the
kitchen. He opened the cupboard. He took out
a measuring cup and two plastic glasses. He
opened the packets.

He put the green crystals in one glass and the
red crystals in the other. He measured eight
ounces of water and poured it into the glass with
the green crystals. They turned into a dark
green liquid.

Then he measured another eight ounces of
water. He poured it into the glass with the red
crystals. They turned into a bright red liquid.

Irving took one glass in each hand. He
walked very slowly and carefully so he wouldn't
spill a drop. He carried the glasses up to his room.

He set the glasses on his desk and took a deep breath. He could hardly wait. In seconds he'd be a real live monster.

He decided to start with just a couple of gulps. He wanted to make the Monster-Ade last as long as possible.

Irving picked up the glass and put it to his lips. Just then the phone rang. He didn't want to answer it. He wanted to ignore it. He wanted to gulp down the green Monster-Ade.

But the phone kept ringing. It might be important. It might even be an emergency.

Irving put down the glass. He went into his parents' bedroom. He picked up the phone.

It was Pete. "Did you get the homework assignment for tonight?" he asked.

"I got something a lot better than that," said Irving.

"What?" Pete asked.

"Monster-Ade!" Irving replied.

"You're kidding!"

Irving told Pete about how Claire had hidden the package. He told him about the instructions and the crystals.

"Did you try it yet?" Pete asked.

"I was just going to when the phone rang."

"Bet it won't work," Pete scoffed

"Come over, then. You can watch me turn into a monster before your eyes."

"*If* the stuff works. But it won't."

"Do you want to see me try it, or don't you?" Irving demanded.

"I guess so," Pete said.

"Then hurry up," Irving told him. "Everything's ready. I'm not going to wait for long."

"Okay, okay," Pete replied. "I'm on my way. Don't do anything till I get there."

Irving hung up the phone and went back into his bedroom. The glass of red liquid was still on the desk. But the glass of green liquid was missing.

Irving ran out into the hall and opened his sister's bedroom door. Claire was drinking from a plastic glass of green liquid. She tilted the glass on end and licked up the very last drop.

"Claire!" Irving screamed at the top of his lungs.

Claire licked her lips and giggled. "Yum," she said.

6

Irving stared at his sister. Suddenly all her fingernails turned into claws.

Claire's smirk disappeared. She looked puzzled. "What's happen—" she started to ask.

But Claire couldn't finish her sentence. Irving watched as she sprouted an enormous tongue. She curled it up and licked her forehead. Then two enormous fangs sprang out of Claire's upper jaw.

Irving took one step backward. There was no telling what would happen next. After all, the instructions had said a little Monster-Ade would go a long way. And Claire hadn't drunk a little Monster-Ade. She had drunk every last drop.

And it was working! The skin on Claire's hands and face turned all scaly. A gnarled horn sprouted from her forehead. Claire looked at herself in the mirror and giggled—or tried to. What came out instead was a snort—and a little

flame. Then small batlike wings popped through Claire's T-shirt. Irving hoped she wouldn't be able to fly around with them.

No doubt about it, Irving's great Monster-Ade plans had backfired. He just hoped Monstra wouldn't get angry about it.

The doorbell rang. Irving backed into the hall and slammed Claire's door behind him. He ran down the stairs. He let Pete in. He locked the front door.

"What's going on?" Pete demanded.

"Claire just drank all the stuff. That's all."

"Told you it wouldn't work," Pete replied.

A door slammed upstairs. Pete and Irving heard a mighty roar.

"Don't be so sure," Irving said.

At the top of the stairs was a scaly monster. A monster with big long fangs and tiny sharp claws. A monster with ugly batlike wings. A monster with a big gnarled horn. A monster with cute little kittens all over her baby-blue jumper.

"C-C-Claire?" Pete stammered.

Irving nodded grimly. "Monstra."

Monstra snorted and spat fire—in a *friendly* kind of way.

"Uh-oh," Pete said.

Monstra crept down the stairs. She reached out and sharpened her claws on the carpet.

"What are we going to do?" Irving moaned.

"What do you mean, 'we'?" Pete asked. "She's *your* sister."

Monstra scampered past them and sharpened her claws on the sofa.

"Claire!" Irving screamed. "Stop that!"

Monstra just gave a giggly snort and spat fire at him. She ran into the kitchen.

Irving chased after her. "Come on, Pete! You've got to help me."

"Are you kidding? She's a monster. A *real* one! There's no telling what she might do!"

"Just keep an eye on her," Irving said. "Watch where she goes. I'm going upstairs to get the antidote."

"You keep *your* eye on her," Pete said. "*I'll* get the antidote."

"Okay," Irving said. "It's the glass of red stuff on my desk. And bring the blanket from my bed."

"Back in a flash!" said Pete.

"Hurry!" Irving urged. Monstra was rooting around in the refrigerator.

"Nice monster," Irving said pleasantly.

Monstra grabbed a bottle of ketchup from the fridge.

"I'm back," Pete told Irving.

Irving took the blanket. "You hold the antidote," he whispered. "Whatever you do, don't spill it. First we'll catch her and wrap her in the blanket. Then we'll make her take the stuff."

"Oh, *that* sounds easy," Pete scoffed. "Hey, look!"

Monstra put the ketchup bottle to her lips. She turned it upside down like a bottle of soda. She drank it down.

"Gross!" said Pete.

"What does it mean when monsters drink ketchup?" Irving asked him.

"How should I know?" Pete said. "In the movies they always drink blood."

Monstra set down the ketchup bottle. She belched a tiny little flame. Then she scampered down the stairs to the basement.

"Great!" said Irving. "We can trap her down there."

"Or she can trap us," Pete pointed out.

Irving took the bright red fire extinguisher down from the wall. "Just in case she tries anything with that dragon breath. And whatever you do, don't spill that antidote."

"Right," Pete said. "You go first."

7

Irving turned on the basement light and tiptoed down the stairs. Pete stayed right behind him. But Monstra was nowhere to be seen.

"Where is she?" Pete whispered.

Irving heard a snorty giggle. He looked up. Monstra was hanging like a bat from the water pipes on the ceiling.

"Claire!" Irving screamed. "Monstra! You get down from there!"

Monstra shook her head and snort-giggled.

"Right now!" Irving said. "Down!"

Monstra wrinkled up her face and spat a little flame toward him.

"This isn't going to be easy," Pete said.

"You're telling me!" Irving agreed.

"Maybe you can knock her down," Pete said. He pointed to a broom in the corner.

Irving set the fire extinguisher and blanket on the Ping-Pong table. "Come down!" he shouted, poking her with the broom. But Monstra just took a bite out of it. She spat the bristles at Irving and Pete.

"That's not funny!" Irving said. But before he could poke her again, Monstra jumped down to the floor. Then she leaped to the top of the clothes dryer.

"She's in the corner," Irving whispered. "Now we'll get her." He grabbed the blanket and threw it over his monster-sister.

But before he could do anything else, sharp claws turned the blanket to shreds. Monstra leaped up to the water pipes and sneaked away.

"The blanket's burning!" Pete cried. "She must have breathed on it!"

Irving read the directions on the fire extinguisher. He ripped off the red tab. He aimed at the blanket. He squeezed the trigger. There was a loud *whoosh!* Foamy chemicals sprayed all over the blanket. The fire went out.

Monstra watched the whole thing from the ceiling. She giggled and snorted.

"Maybe we should just try being nice," said Irving. "Maybe we should just ask her to drink what's in the glass."

"Might work." Pete shrugged. "Might not."

Irving took the glass from Pete's hands and walked over to his sister. "See?" he said. "Nice red pop. Want some?"

Monstra snort-giggled and shook her head.

Irving pretended to take a sip. "Mmm. Good." Monstra reached down toward the glass.

Irving handed it to her. Monstra sniffed the red liquid. She made a face. Then she threw the glass across the room.

Some of the antidote landed on Irving's head. Some of it made a bright red stain on Pete's white T-shirt. The rest landed on the floor and trickled down the drain. Monstra snort-giggled and jumped onto the Ping-Pong table.

"Uh-oh," said Pete. "Is there any more of that stuff?"

Irving wiped his face and shook his head.

Pete looked at the red mess on his T-shirt. He

went to the laundry sink and tried to rinse off the stain. It didn't come out. "You little monster!" Pete shouted. "Are you ever going to get it when your mom and dad come home!"

Irving shuddered. He had the sinking feeling *he* was going to be the one who was going to get it when his mom and dad came home. What would they think when he told them his sister had turned into a real fire-breathing monster— and that all the antidote had gone down the drain?

Monstra just snort-giggled and took a nibble of the Ping-Pong net.

8

Pete and Irving went up the stairs and locked the basement door behind them. "At least she can't do too much damage down there," Pete said.

"Right," Irving said sarcastically. "All she can do is eat up the Ping-Pong table, the washer, the dryer, the hot-water heater, and the furnace. And set fire to the house."

"Good luck," Pete said. "I'm out of here." And he was gone.

Irving looked out the window. His parents' car was coming up the driveway. He tried to think of a good way to break the news. This was going to be trouble. No doubt about it.

Irving heard a noise from the kitchen. It sounded like claws scratching at a basement door.

"Hi," Mr. Shapiro said cheerfully. "What's new?"

Irving squirmed. "Nothing much."

Mrs. Shapiro handed him a big, flat pizza box. "Because you've been so good to Claire, we bought your favorite," she said. "Mushrooms, pepperoni, onions, and extra garlic. The bad-breath special."

Usually Irving would have said "Great!" But tonight he didn't feel too enthusiastic. In fact, he felt like crawling into a hole and hiding.

"What happened to the couch?" Mrs. Shapiro shrieked.

Irving stalled. "Huh?"

Mrs. Shapiro scowled. "This whole side is clawed to shreds. Who did that?"

"Monstra," Irving replied.

"Irving, how many times have we told you not to call your sister that?" demanded Mrs. Shapiro.

"And what's that scratching noise I hear?" asked Mr. Shapiro.

Irving played dumb. "What scratching noise?"

"In the kitchen," said Mr. Shapiro.

He went to look. Irving and his mom followed. "It's coming from behind the basement door," Mr. Shapiro said.

"Did you bring home a cat?" Irving's mother asked suspiciously.

Irving shook his head. The scratching grew frantic.

"You didn't bring home some wild animal, did you?" demanded Mrs. Shapiro.

Irving sighed. "It's kind of complicated."

There was a loud roar from behind the door. "Did you bring home something dangerous?" demanded Irving's father.

"No," Irving explained. "That's Monstra—I mean Claire!"

"Irving, how could you!" shrieked his mother. "We've told you a hundred times never to lock anyone in there—or in closets or anyplace else."

"Irving, that's terrible!" his father agreed. "You open that door and let her out right this minute!"

"I've got to tell you something first," Irving said.

There was a loud roar. "I'm going to tell *you* a few things if you don't open that door right now," said Mr. Shapiro.

"But, Dad—" Irving stammered.

"No buts. I'm counting three. One . . ."

Irving shook his head. He wanted to warn his parents, but the words wouldn't come out.

"Two . . ."

Another loud roar.

"Three," Irving said wearily. He opened the door.

Monstra leaped onto the kitchen table, looked around, and giggle-snorted. She took a bite out of a banana—skin and all.

"Claire?" her mother gasped.

Monstra smiled with all her teeth and fangs.

9

"**H**ow did this happen?" Mrs. Shapiro demanded.

"I always said she was a little monster," Irving replied.

"Somehow I don't think that's the whole story," Mr. Shapiro said.

Monstra grunted, shook her head back and forth, and pointed accusingly at Irving.

"Maybe it was something she ate?"

Monstra roared even louder.

"Enough roaring!" Irving screamed. "I confess!" And he told his parents all about the Monster-Ade.

"Monster-Ade!" exclaimed Mrs. Shapiro. "How could you do this to your little sister?"

"I didn't do it to her," Irving protested. "She did it to herself. I bought the stuff to turn *me* into a monster. I turned my back for one lousy second, and she stole it."

36

Monstra stuck out her tongue at him and spat a tiny flame. "All right, Claire," said Mrs. Shapiro. "That's enough out of you."

"Are you sure there's no more of the antidote?" Mr. Shapiro asked.

"Down the drain," Irving said. "Every last drop."

"Well, we have to get more," said his father. "Bring me the box. I'll straighten this out."

Irving trudged upstairs. He trudged down again with the Monster-Ade package and handed it to his father.

Mr. Shapiro looked at the package and shook his head. "The things they sell today! And to kids, too!" he clucked. "Well, here's the phone number. I'll call the company and find out how to change Claire back. And guess who's going to pay for the long-distance call?"

Irving pointed to himself.

"Right you are, sonny boy," said Mr. Shapiro. He picked up the phone and dialed the number on the order form.

Irving just hoped the call wouldn't last too long. After spending ten dollars of his life's savings on Monster-Ade, there wasn't a whole lot left for phone calls.

Mr. Shapiro frowned and hung up. "What did they say?" Irving asked.

"I got a recording," his Dad replied. "The office is closed for the evening."

"What should we do now?" Mrs. Shapiro wanted to know.

Irving's father looked thoughtful. "We don't have a lot of choices. We'll just have to make the best of things until tomorrow."

"Maybe the stuff will wear out," Irving said.

"Not in any hurry," Mr. Shapiro replied thoughtfully. "These instructions say to drink only a little at a time. You said Claire drank it *all.*"

Monstra rolled over, smiled, and dug her claws into the sofa. "Claire!" her mother scolded.

Monstra frowned and spat a tiny little flame.

"And no back talk!" Mrs. Shapiro warned.

"Why don't you set the table, Irving?" asked Mr. Shapiro. "We may as well have dinner."

Monstra grunted and snuffled happily.

"But it's Claire's turn to set the table," Irving protested.

"Too bad," said Mrs. Shapiro. "I don't want her clawing around in the silverware drawer. Or the cupboards."

Monstra smiled and scratched her horn.

Irving put out knives and forks and plates and glasses and napkins. "Okay," he called out. "The table's set."

With a loud grunt Monstra bounded in from the living room and reached toward the pizza. "Claire!" her mother shouted. "Where are your manners?"

Irving leaned over and pushed her away. "Come on, Claire. You'll get some in a second."

Monstra roared and spat a tiny flame. She flashed her claws. "See?" said Irving. "It's just like always around here. No difference at all."

"Very funny," said Mr. Shapiro. He handed Monstra a plate with a slice of pizza on it.

Monstra sniffed at the pizza, nudged it with her horn, and stuck it on her claws. Then she sucked the whole slice into her mouth and swallowed it in one gulp.

"Yuck!" Irving shouted.

"Claire, how many times have your father and I told you to chew your food?" said Mrs. Shapiro.

Monstra giggle-snorted. She belched fire. Then she pointed to the pizza that was left.

"You're just going to have to wait until the rest of us are served," Mrs. Shapiro said.

But Monstra didn't wait. She stuck her big paws into the box and tore off half the pizza. She dangled it over her mouth and inhaled it bit by bit.

"Yuck!" said Irving. "Gross!"

"You'd better grab a slice before Claire gets it all," Mr. Shapiro said.

Irving reached into the box and tugged at the

pizza. But a claw pricked his finger. He pulled his hand back.

Monstra giggled wildly. She took the rest of the pizza out of the box.

"Claire, give that back to your brother. Right now!" shouted Mr. Shapiro.

Monstra shook her head.

"I'm warning you," said her father. "One . . . two . . ."

When her father cried "Three!" Monstra put the pizza back in the box. But first she stuck out her long tongue and licked it all over.

"Yuck—monster germs!" Irving cried.

"Claire, you are being very bad," said Mrs. Shapiro.

Monstra hung her head and snuffled. She seemed to be very sorry for what she had done.

"Bad?" Irving snorted. "If I did that, I'd lose my allowance for a month."

"Because you're old enough to know better," said Mr. Shapiro.

Five claws began sneaking toward the pizza box.

"So is Claire!" Irving protested.

"This time I would have to agree with you," said Mr. Shapiro, "if it weren't for the fact that she's a monster. I'm not sure how monsters behave at Claire's age."

Monstra yanked the box off the table and into her lap.

"Claire!" her mother scolded.

"Claire!" her father shouted.

"Monstra!" Irving hollered.

Monstra ignored them. She wolfed down the rest of the pizza. She ate the box. Then she swallowed her napkin and belched a little flame of satisfaction.

"What's for dessert?" said Irving. "The newspaper?"

"Don't give her any ideas," said Mrs. Shapiro.

"I'm hungry!" Irving complained. "What's for supper?"

But nobody answered him. Monstra bit into her plastic placemat. It was too tough for her sensitive fangs.

Irving's mother whisked it away. Monstra

growled in protest. Suddenly she began gasping and wheezing and waving her arms in the air.

"What's wrong?" her mother asked.

"I think she's going to be sick," said Irving.

Irving was right.

10

Mr. Shapiro parked the car in the hospital parking lot. Irving was very glad to get out. All the way to the hospital, Monstra had grunted and snorted and wheezed and flashed her claws and spat little flames at him—and her breath wasn't exactly sweet.

The Shapiros went through a door marked EMERGENCY ENTRANCE and walked up to a receptionist's desk. "That's a very cute costume, little girl," said a friendly woman. She patted Monstra on the horn. "What seems to be the trouble?"

Monstra growled and snorted.

"Our daughter is sick to her stomach," Mr. Shapiro explained.

"That doesn't sound like a real emergency," the receptionist said. "There are a lot of very sick people ahead of you. You'll have a long wait."

"But there's another problem," Mr. Shapiro said. "Our daughter has turned into a monster."

The receptionist smiled. "I know exactly what you mean. My daughter can be quite a monster herself."

"But Claire really *is* a monster," said Mrs. Shapiro. "Show your fangs, dear."

"And belch some fire," Mr. Shapiro added.

Monstra did.

The receptionist got up from her desk and took two steps back. "I'll have to ask you to leave."

"Great!" Irving muttered. "I'm starving." His father gave him a dirty look.

"This is a hospital for humans—not for dogs, cats, gerbils, roosters, or cockatoos. Or monsters," the receptionist said.

"But Claire's human," Mr. Shapiro protested.

"Oh, really!" the receptionist sniffed.

Monstra scratched her horn and growled.

"Well, she used to be," said Mrs. Shapiro. "Before *this* happened."

"Why don't you try the veterinary hospital?"

said the receptionist. "I'm sure they'll be happy to treat this little . . . creature."

There was nothing more to discuss. The Shapiros left the hospital and got back into their car.

The animal hospital was packed with patients—dogs on leashes, cats in carriers, birds in cages, and a weasel on a rope. They were all pretty calm until Claire "Monstra" Shapiro walked through the door.

A big German shepherd barked. An orange cat yowled and hissed. A parrot screeched. The weasel jumped on his owner's shoulder and chittered. Monstra bared her fangs, flashed her claws, and roared.

"What is that beast?" a large woman demanded.

"It's scaring poor Popcorn!" cried a bald man with a yipping Chihuahua.

"Don't let it near me or Jonesy!" shrieked an old woman, gathering up her frightened kitten.

Monstra spat a long tongue of flame. The whole room went wild with barking, bellowing, yipping, and howling.

A man with a white lab coat came through a doorway. His badge said ASSISTANT.

"Calm down, calm down, everybody," he said soothingly. "Is there a problem?"

"That . . . *thing* is the problem," said the bald man. He pointed to Monstra.

"Everybody, just take it easy," said the assistant. "Do you have an appointment?" he asked the Shapiros.

"No," said Irving's dad. "It's an emergency."

"What kind of emergency?" the assistant asked.

Mr. Shapiro pointed to Monstra. She smiled, bared her fangs, and purred.

"She looks pretty healthy to me," the assistant said. "Just what kind of animal is she?"

"She's no animal," Mrs. Shapiro said indignantly. "She's our daughter."

"Many people feel that way about their pets," said the assistant. "But I need to know what kind of animal she is."

Mr. Shapiro shrugged. "Human."

The assistant was beginning to lose his patience. "This is an *animal* hospital."

"Humans are animals," Irving piped up. "Especially Claire."

Monstra stuck out her tongue and spat a flame at him.

"But we don't treat humans," the assistant said firmly. "It's not allowed."

"Not even if they've been turned into monsters?" Mr. Shapiro asked.

"*Especially* not if they've been turned into monsters," said the assistant. "I'm scared of monsters. And so are our patients."

Suddenly one of the dogs began to snarl. Monstra roared back. The cats and dogs and birds joined in the racket.

Mr. Shapiro put his arm on Monstra's left wing and steered her out the door. Monstra happily licked her horn. She didn't seem sick anymore.

"Monstra looks okay," Irving said. "You know what we need?"

"What we need is for certain young men to stop trying to turn their sisters into horrible beasts," said his mom.

"What we need is food," said Irving. "I'm starving!"

"We'll stop and get a bag of Chick-a-burgers," said Mrs. Shapiro.

Monstra grunted and licked her lips.

"None for you," Irving said. "You ate everybody else's dinner, and you got sick besides."

Monstra snarled and growled.

The Chick-a-burgers were cold by the time the Shapiros got home. But Monstra didn't get her paws on them, even though she seemed to be hungry.

Monstra had to sleep in the bathtub so she couldn't accidentally set fire to her bed. When Irving woke up in the middle of the night, he decided to check up on her.

Monstra wasn't asleep. She was busy catching a cockroach. She trapped it in her furry paw. Then she ate it.

11

"I just spoke with the Monster-Ade people," said Mr. Shapiro at breakfast the next morning. "They're sending the antidote by air express. It should be here tonight."

"You'll have to go to preschool with Claire today," Mrs. Shapiro told Irving. "To keep an eye on her."

"She should stay home sick!" Irving protested.

"She isn't sick," said his dad. "Are you, Claire?"

Monstra smiled, snort-giggled, and crunched on a bagel.

"But she's a monster!" Irving protested. "And monsters don't go to preschool."

"She may be a monster, but she's still your little sister," said Mrs. Shapiro. "And that's that."

"Phooey! I'm not going to sit in Claire's class with all the little kids."

52

"Oh, yes, you are," said Mr. Shapiro. "Do I need to remind you who started this whole thing?"

"No." Irving sighed. "Can I put her on a leash?"

"A leash?" exclaimed Mrs. Shapiro. "She's your sister—not your dog!"

"But she's not just any sister. She's Monstra!"

Monstra growled and snarled.

Mrs. Shapiro turned to her and spoke in a very stern voice. "Claire, you have to be on your very best behavior in school today. No snarling. No growling. And especially no biting. Do you understand?"

Monstra nodded.

"This is going to be terrible," Irving muttered. "I just know it."

Irving's mom drove them to Claire's preschool. Irving took his sister straight to the principal's office.

"Pets are not allowed in school," the principal's secretary said before he could get a word in edgewise. "No exceptions. And aren't you a little old to be a student here?"

"I'm not a student here. Claire is," Irving replied. "And she's not a pet. She's my sister."

Monstra snort-giggled. The secretary looked her in the eye. "She does look kind of familiar."

Irving handed the secretary a note from his parents. "Very interesting," she muttered. "Let's see what the principal has to say about this."

"Now be nice," Irving whispered to Monstra while they waited. "Don't snap at him or anything, okay?"

Monstra nodded and purred.

"Is this little monster really Claire?" the principal asked.

"Yes," Irving replied. "My mom wants me to go to school with her. Just to make sure she doesn't get in trouble."

"Good idea," said the principal. He handed the note back to Irving. "Be sure you show this to the teacher. And take good care of your little monster."

Monstra loved preschool. She couldn't wait to get to class. But the instant she and Irving stepped through the classroom door, a loud murmur rose from the group.

"What's that?" shouted one of the kids.

"Oooh! It's a monster!" hollered another.

"Hey!" shrieked a third. "It's Claire! She's wearing that cute hair ribbon! Hi, Claire!"

Monstra snort-giggled and waved hello.

"Simmer down!" shouted the teacher. The whole class kept talking about Monstra, but not quite as noisily.

"What is going on?" the teacher asked Irving.

He handed her the note. "If it's okay with the principal," the teacher said, "it's okay with me. But if there's any trouble, out she goes. You two can sit in the back of the room."

Irving led his sister past the other kids. She kept waving hello. "Great costume!" one kid said.

"And it's not even Halloween!" said another.

Irving wanted to read a book, but he didn't

dare take his eyes off Monstra for even a second. Kids kept turning around to stare at her. Monstra waved and giggle-snorted back.

Snack time was hard. Irving had to grab the milk carton from Monstra's paws to keep her from eating it. He had to snatch up the cookie plate to keep Monstra from wolfing down every last chocolate chip. And after she wiped her horn, he had to make sure she didn't eat her napkin.

Then the whole class cut patterns from construction paper. But no matter how hard she tried, Monstra couldn't get the little plastic scissors to fit her paws. She got so frustrated, she spat a little burst of flame that set fire to the paper.

Irving made her drop it. He stamped it out with his foot.

"Thank you, Irving," said the teacher. "But one more incident like that, and we'll have to send your sister back to the principal's office. Do you understand, Claire?"

Monstra nodded and grunted.

Everything was fine for a while. The class sang some songs, and Monstra snorted along. The class did some exercises, and Monstra showed off by hanging from the door frame. The class drew pictures, and Monstra made some scribbles with a blue crayon she stuck in her paw.

Then the teacher shouted "Alphabet time!" She put a tray of plastic letters in the middle of the circle of kids. Every pupil grabbed one letter and shouted out its name.

But Monstra couldn't shout. She could only roar. And when she grabbed the letter *R*, she treated it like a cookie. She bit off one of its legs and turned it into a *P*. Then she swallowed the rest of the letter.

There was nothing Irving could do. The class howled with laughter. "Out!" said the teacher. Monstra calmly picked up the *O* and ate that, too. Then she and Irving headed for the principal's office.

12

The principal made Irving take Monstra home. Usually Irving loved days off from school. But this time it was no fun at all.

Irving made Monstra a tuna-fish sandwich for lunch. First she toasted it with her flame-breath. Then she poured a whole glass of milk over it. Finally she ate it. Irving couldn't stand to watch.

Later she sneaked into his bedroom and sharpened her claws on his space-shuttle bedspread. It took Irving a lot of talking and fifteen pecan cookies to get her to stop. Finally he convinced her to take a nap in the bathtub.

Pete came by after school. "Did you get the antidote yet?" he asked.

A loud roar came down from upstairs. "Three guesses," Irving said.

"Great!" Pete replied. "Then there's still time!"

"For what?"

"A sideshow. A circus. With Monstra as the star."

Irving thought it over. "I don't know. . . ."

"Come on!" Pete urged. "We can make money. I already told everybody at school about Monstra. They're dying to see her."

"But she's not a circus act," Irving said. "She's my little sister."

"She looks pretty monstrous to me," Pete reminded him.

"Yeah, but maybe she doesn't want everybody staring at her and making fun of her. How would *you* like it?"

"I don't know. *I'm* not a monster."

Irving heard shouts of "Where's Monstra?" and "We want Monstra!" He looked outside. It seemed as though every kid in Irving's school was coming toward the Shapiros' house.

Pete opened the door and stuck his head out. "Hold your horses!" he shouted. "Make a line outside the garage! You'll all get your turn!"

He shut the door. "See? What did I tell you? I say we charge half a dollar. We'll split it fifty-fifty."

Irving thought it over. "I don't know. . . ."

"Come on. Nobody's going to hurt her or anything."

"Oh, all right," Irving said. "You go out there and talk to the crowd. I'll bring Monstra down to the garage."

Irving ran up the stairs and opened the bathroom door. But Monstra wasn't there.

"Claire!" he shouted. "Monstra! Where are you?"

Suddenly he heard kids outside oohing and aahing. He ran to his parents' bedroom and looked out the window. Monstra was out on the porch roof, bellowing at the crowd.

Five pecan cookies later, Irving lured Monstra back inside. Five more cookies got her down to the garage. Irving began to wonder if this circus was such a good idea after all.

Through the garage door, Irving heard Pete

drumming up business. "See Monstra spit fire! See Monstra bare her fangs! See her wings! See her claws! See the monster that just yesterday was Claire Shapiro, Irving's little sister!"

"Okay!" somebody shouted. "We all paid our money! Let's see her!"

"Open the door, Irving!" Pete shouted.

"I can't," Irving yelled. "She's up near the ceiling and growling at me! And she's got the garage-door opener!"

"Everybody's waiting!" Pete hollered. "Get it back!"

"I'm trying!"

"Try harder!" Pete said. "Get a ladder or something. I've got almost thirty dollars out here!"

"Come on, Claire," Irving coaxed his sister. "Come down from up there."

Monstra spat a little flame in his direction. She squeezed the garage-door opener tighter in her hand—and accidentally pressed the button.

Like the curtain on a stage, the garage door

rolled up into the air. A startled Monstra stood on her perch at the back of the empty garage. She hissed at the crowd.

"Come on in," Irving told the kids. "But be careful. She might accidentally send the door down again."

"She's the eighth wonder of the world!" Pete proclaimed. "The monster girl! There's nothing like her anywhere else on earth!"

"Let's see her do those tricks!" somebody shouted. "Let's see her breathe fire!"

Monstra just flapped her wings and roared.

"We haven't really got her trained yet," Pete apologized. "She's only been a monster since yesterday."

Irving tried to coax Monstra down from her perch. "Come on, Claire."

Monstra shook her head and snuffled.

"Come on, Monstra!" shouted somebody in the crowd. "Do something monstrous!"

Monstra roared and bared her fangs.

"More!" someone cried.

Monstra flashed her claws and belched an enormous flame.

"Do it again!" someone shouted.

But Monstra was getting annoyed. She leaped down from her perch and started roaring at the crowd. "Calm down, Claire," her brother said. "Nobody's trying to hurt you."

"Yeah," Pete agreed. "Cool out a little."

But Monstra was moving toward the crowd. "Nice Monstra," the kids at the front said nervously.

"She won't hurt us, will she?" someone shouted.

"I hope not," Irving squeaked. "I think she's afraid of you. Maybe you should go home now."

Monstra spat a tiny flame and stuck out her tongue.

"Give us our money back!" one kid shouted. "You said she'd do all kinds of tricks."

Monstra roared and flashed her claws.

"I've seen plenty!" another kid cried. "I'm going home. Out of my way!"

Monstra roared and spat more fire. The crowd turned and hurried out of the garage. Irving grabbed the garage-door opener and pressed the button. The door slammed shut.

"I told you that wasn't such a great idea," Irving said.

"Sure it was!" Pete exclaimed. He counted the money into two piles on a shelf at the end of the garage. "We made twenty-eight dollars—fourteen apiece!"

Just then Monstra jumped up on the shelf, bared her claws, and roared at Pete.

"I wonder why she's in such a bad mood," he said.

"Probably hungry again," said Irving.

"Look!" Pete cried. With one big scoop of her paw, Monstra gathered up all the coins and bills. In two big bites, she ate up every one of them.

"All our money! Gone!" Pete moaned.

"I warned you," Irving said. "I told you this was a bad idea."

With a huge gulp, Monstra swallowed what

she'd been chewing. Then she giggle-snorted and started purring.

Irving shook his head. "I guess she *was* hungry."

Then Irving heard the doorbell. He ran through the house to answer it. The man outside was wearing a uniform and a baseball cap. Both said INSTANT EXPRESS.

Irving opened the door. The deliveryman said, "Will you sign for this package? It's for Mr. Herman Shapiro."

"Irving, get back here fast!" Pete shouted. "The little monster is up near the ceiling again—and she's eating an old tire!"

"In a minute!" Irving shouted back. He looked at the package. It was from Transylvania, Kentucky.

13

"Irving, hurry up!" Pete hollered. "Your sister just ate a whole cobweb—and the spider, too!"

"I'll be there in a minute!" Irving shouted back. He signed for the package, thanked the deliveryman, and rushed back to the garage. "We got it! The antidote!"

"About time," Pete said. Monstra was staring at a little hole in the wall and trying to wiggle her paw inside.

Irving opened the package. There were two packets of red crystals inside.

"I wonder if this stuff will make her throw up," Pete said. "Maybe we can get some of our money back."

Irving scanned the instructions:

Monster-Ade Antidote

Even if you are *desperate*, please take a moment to read these important instructions:

    I. Mix one packet well with one cup (eight ounces) of water.

2. To stop being a monster, drink the antidote. Drink at least as much as you drank of **Monster-Ade**. In seconds you should return to normal.

Thank you for using this fine **Monster-Ade** product.

"Help me catch her and give her the stuff," Irving said.

"Not me!" Pete scoffed. "I got enough of that antidote on my T-shirt last time. And it doesn't wash out, either!"

"Come on," Irving begged. "Please?"

"Okay. But only if you let me borrow your raincoat."

Pete and Irving locked Monstra in the garage. Irving mixed up the antidote. Then he took the extra packet of crystals upstairs and hid it at the very back of his top dresser drawer, where Monstra would never find it—just in case. "Ready?" he asked.

Pete fastened the hood on Irving's raincoat. "Ready!"

Irving opened the door to the garage. Monstra was in a corner, munching on something gray and furry.

"Yuck" said Pete. "Mouseburgers! Maybe she'll throw up even without the antidote!"

"Let's just hope she's thirsty," Irving said. "Claire, do you want a nice red soft drink?"

Monstra just grunted.

"Come on, Claire," Irving coaxed, showing her the glass. "How about a nice cool drink?"

Monstra looked sort of interested. Irving moved closer. "Here you go. Now stand up and have a sip."

Monstra eyed the glass suspiciously.

"It's delicious," Irving said. He pretended to take a drink. He licked his lips. "Yum."

Monstra stood up and reached out. Irving handed her the glass.

"Batten down the hatches!" Pete cried. He opened Irving's umbrella.

Monstra stuck her nose into the glass and sniffed it suspiciously. She took a tiny sip. She smiled. She drank the rest of the antidote down

in one big gulp. Then she took a huge bite out
of the glass and swallowed that, too.

"Claire!" Irving shouted. He grabbed the
glass before she could eat the rest of it.

Pete peeked out from under the umbrella.
"Did she drink it?"

"Yeah," Irving said.

"Nothing's happening," Pete remarked.

"Yeah," Irving said. "I wonder what's wrong."

Suddenly Monstra grabbed her stomach and
gave a horrible groan. Her batlike wings

shriveled up and disappeared. The horn on her forehead twisted around and vanished into thin air. Her scaly arms and legs turned into skin again. Her claws became plain old fingernails. Her fangs popped back into regular teeth.

Claire giggled without even a trace of a snort. She stuck out her plain old human tongue. And she didn't breathe a bit of fire.

Irving felt happy to see his little sister instead of Monstra. "Claire!" he exclaimed. "You're normal again!"

Claire just giggled.

"What was it like?" Pete asked.

"What?" Claire said.

"You know," Irving told her. "Being a monster."

"Scary." Claire giggled.

"I'll say," Pete agreed.

Claire made a face. "My tummy hurts."

"No kidding!" Pete muttered.

"Maybe this time you'll learn your lesson," Irving said sternly.

Claire just smiled.

"Maybe you'll stop being so much of a monster," Irving added.

Claire just giggled and went through the door. Pete and Irving followed her as far as the kitchen.

"Well, your parents ought to be happy," Pete said.

Irving sighed. "Yeah."

"It *was* kind of interesting."

"Yeah, but *I* was the one who was supposed to be the monster," Irving reminded him. "I was the one who was supposed to have all the fun."

Just then he heard loud noises above his head. "Come on!" he told Pete. They rushed upstairs to his bedroom.

Claire was shouting, singing, and jumping up and down on Irving's bed. She was trying to work Irving's special yo-yo at the same time, but she was all tangled up in the string. She was wearing Irving's tape player on her jumper and his headphones over her ears. "Claire!" Irving screamed. "Stop it!"

But Claire didn't stop. She kept shouting and singing and jumping.

Irving and Pete grabbed her by the feet. Then they untangled her from the yo-yo string and the headphone cord.

"Irving!" Mrs. Shapiro hollered. "Is everything okay up there?"

Claire slipped away from Irving and Pete. She ran downstairs to greet her parents.

Irving didn't bother. He could hear how happy everybody was down there. But he wasn't happy anymore. Not one bit.

"Maybe you should give her the rest of the antidote." Pete laughed.

Irving just grunted.

"Maybe you should order more Monster-Ade for yourself," Pete joked.

Irving stared at himself in the mirror. He tried to imagine what he'd look like with big long fangs and sharp shiny claws and ugly batlike wings and a huge gnarled horn.

"Pete," he said, "can you lend me ten dollars?"